The Crash

A novel by

Paul Kropp

HIP-JR.

HIP Junior
Copyright © 2005 by High Interest Publishing

Library and Archives Canada Cataloguing in Publication

Kropp, Paul, 1948-
    The crash / Paul Kropp.

(HIP jr)
ISBN 1-897039-12-3

I. Title. II. Series.

PS8571.R772C73 2005   jC813'.54   C2005-905370-4

General editor: Paul Kropp
Text design and typesetting: Laura Brady
Illustrations drawn by: Catherine Doherty
Cover design: Robert Corrigan

3 4 5 6 7   13 12

Printed and bound in Canada

A school bus slides off a cliff in a snowstorm. The bus driver is out cold. One of the guys is badly hurt. Can Craig, Rory and Lerch find help in time?

CHAPTER 1

The Wheels on the Bus

After the game, we had to wait out in front of the school. That's when we saw our old school bus slide on the ice. It was kind of funny. The big yellow bus seemed to be skating on the school parking lot.

"Hey, the bus is doing a donut," I yelled.

"A double donut," Ben said.

"The wheels on the bus go skid, skid, skid . . ." Rory sang. It was that little-kid song with new words.

We all began to laugh. The big bus was doing a real skid, the back end going out to one side. There was only one other car in the lot, so the skid was no big deal. In a second, the bus driver got control back.

"That was funny, man," Rory said.

"Yeah, almost as funny as that last basket you missed," I told him.

Then we laughed again, this time at Rory. We had just finished a basketball game. The other team beat us, not badly, but they beat us. The final score was 66–62, and that's what hurt. If Rory's pass had got to me . . . but it didn't. We lost the ball and they sunk two baskets, real quick. By then it was all over.

"If you could catch, Craig," Rory said.

"If you could aim, you loser," I shot back.

"Maybe you guys should both shut up," Big Ben told us. "I'm beat. All I want to do is get home."

So we shut up. Big Ben was the real leader of our team. He was bigger than Rory and me, though he was only 12, and he scored the most points. He had sunk 30 of our 62 points. Maybe if Rory had passed to him at the end, we would have won. But Rory passed to me. I missed the catch, so we lost. Still, I wasn't going to admit all that to Rory.

There were four of us in that parking lot. Big Ben wasn't that tall, but he was our team captain. He was fast on his feet and had a wicked jump shot. Lerch was our centre. He was tall and skinny, and good with long shots. But Lerch had no jump shot or hook, and his ball handling stunk. Up close to the net, he was awful.

Rory and me were guards. Rory is a little short to be a very good basketball player. When the big forward on the other team got set for a shot, Rory couldn't reach his hands. Maybe that's why Rory took so many fouls. He was a fighter, that guy.

And me, I'm Craig, the other guard. Most of my shots are pretty good, but I'm not good at passing or catching. It was my lousy catch that cost us the game. I'll never play NBA, I can tell you that right now.

There were other guys on our team, but they got picked up by their parents. Lucky guys. The four of us had to wait in the cold and take the late school bus. That old bus was skidding across the parking lot. It pulled to a stop in front of us.

"Nice donut, Mrs. D," Rory said.

"Way cool," Lerch told her.

"Looked like fun," I added.

"Enough with the comments," Mrs. D shouted down. Mrs. Davin was the best bus driver our school had. She was cool, but she didn't take any lip. "You kids want to go home or should I leave you here? Maybe you want to freeze to death, eh?" Then she started to close the bus door.

Mrs. Davin can be like that. If you drive a school bus, you learn how to shut kids down. I remember once, back in grade 3, she kicked some big kid right out the school bus door. I mean, she really kicked him! The kid landed on his hands and knees. Let me tell you, he never gave Mrs. D a hard time again.

"These guys will shut up," Ben told her. "Trust me." That was the thing about Ben — when he said "trust me," you just had to trust him.

"Okay, let's go," replied Mrs. D. "The news said we might have a big storm tonight, so I want to get home. It's icy even now." Mrs. D closed the door after we got in. Then she asked the big question. "By the way, did you guys win?"

"Almost," I said.

"It was close," Ben agreed.

"It's all because Craig can't catch . . . " Rory added.

Mrs. D laughed and put the bus into gear. "I don't want to hear it," she groaned. "Maybe next week you'll do better."

The bus *splooshed* its way out of the parking lot. I know *splooshed* isn't a real word. It's the sound you get when a school bus is going through slush. *Sploosh.*

We didn't talk that much on the bus. Ben shot me a nasty look when I opened my mouth. Mrs. D seemed to have a hard time staying on the road. She had the windshield wipers on high, but they didn't help much. It was really hard to see.

Outside, the snow was coming down in big fat flakes. You could see the snow piling up on trees and rooftops. It was all kind of pretty, if you like that kind of winter scene. The trouble was that the snow and slush made it hard to drive.

Inside, the bus was getting warm. Rory took off his jacket and threw it behind him. The rest of us unzipped our coats and got ready for a long ride.

Pretty soon, we came up behind a truck. It was a big Mack semi that sprayed slush from its tires.

Meanwhile, the school bus was getting kind of hot and sticky inside. Our windows were fogged up inside and slushed up outside.

"Pretty nice drive," Rory joked.

"Yeah, real nice," mumbled Mrs. D. She rubbed at the windshield to clear away some fog. "I think we're going to be stuck behind that truck all the way."

The route to our houses was a long one. Rory lived on a farm about twenty minutes from the school. The rest of us were in a little group of houses about ten minutes farther. And that was on a *good* driving day. Now we were moving over the hills behind a truck, in a snowstorm. It would be a long time before we got home for dinner.

Ben yawned. "Pardon me while I take a little nap," he said, yawning again. Then he lay down on a couple of seats.

"Yeah, well, I'm going to study math," Rory said.

That made me laugh. First, it was so dark that you couldn't see a book if you tried. Second, Rory never studied anything. Coach was afraid he might flunk his way off the team.

Lerch was just staring out the windows.

"Guess that leaves me, Mrs. D," I told her. "I'll help you drive." I had been studying my driver's handbook for months. Only four years to go. A guy can't start too soon.

"Just what I need," she said back to me. "A night like this and . . . "

Then it all went crazy. In maybe two seconds, it all went crazy.

CHAPTER 2

Over the Edge

Suddenly the back end of the school bus began skidding. I got thrown into Lerch, who was on my right side. I grabbed the front handrail to hold on to something.

Up in front, Mrs. D was pumping the brake pedal like crazy. She was trying to steer into the skid. That's what they tell you in the driver's handbook — steer into the skid. But the skid was taking us across the road. If another car had been coming...

But it wasn't another car that got us — it was the hill.

"Hold on!" screamed Mrs. D.

I gripped the handrail as hard as I could while the bus slid and bumped across the road and back again. Then there was the scream of metal crunching metal. We hit the metal guard rail beside the road. If we were in a car, the rail would have bounced us back.

But we were in a school bus. We smashed over the guard rail and the bus tipped sideways.

I could feel our side of the bus lift up. For a second, Lerch and I were way down low, Ben and Rory were way up high. Mrs. D was hanging onto the steering wheel like crazy.

Then we began sliding. The school bus was tipped on its right side and we were sliding down the hill. I held on to the rail for all I was worth. My weight pushed me against Lerch. Together we just held on.

The thumps began. The school bus would hit something — a bush or a rock — and the whole bus would shake. For a few seconds, it seemed like we were picking up speed. Then we smashed into something big. Wham! The whole bus flipped around, front to back.

And then it was quiet.

After the awful noise of crashing metal and bouncing down the hill, the silence was good. There was only the hiss of the bus now. For a few seconds, it had all stopped.

Rory was the first person to speak. "What a ride, man!"

Then Lerch groaned, "My arm!"

I grunted something too. At least three of us could talk.

"Ben?" I called out. "Ben, are you all right?"

There was no answer. The bus was pretty dark. I could feel that Lerch was still beside me. I looked over and saw Rory behind the driver's seat. That's where Ben had been sitting too, but now he was gone.

"Ben!" I yelled out.

"He's up there!" Lerch said, pointing.

Ben was in the stairwell of the bus. He must have been thrown there when we flipped on our side. Now he looked like he was asleep on the steps.

In a second, the three of us were out of our seats. Rory actually fell out because his side of the bus was up in the air. It was just good luck that he hadn't sailed out of his seat in the crash.

Ben hadn't been so lucky. His skin was white and there was a big slice across his head. Ben must have sailed into the dashboard headfirst. He got cut on something and must have smashed his head, too. Now the bruise was starting to swell.

"Hey, man, wake up!" I said. "You've got to get up!"

"He's bleeding," Lerch yelled. "Where's that stupid first aid kit?"

I've been taking school buses all my life. You'd think I'd know where the first aid kit was, but I drew a blank. Of course, the bus was on its side, so it was all pretty strange. And maybe I wasn't thinking all that well. My blood was pumping so fast but my brain felt so slow.

"Mrs. D, we need the first aid kit," Rory shouted. Then we all looked up at the driver's seat.

I sucked in my breath.

Mrs. D was out cold. She was still in the driver's seat, held in by her seatbelt, but her face had smashed forward. Now there was blood dripping off the steering wheel. A few drops had already fallen down on me.

Lerch's face turned white. "What are we going to do?"

I didn't say anything. Up above Mrs. D I saw the Red Cross sign. I opened the panel and there it was — the first aid kit. I reached up, grabbed the kit, and pulled it down.

"Okay, where's a bandage?" Rory said. He was talking to himself, I think. "We need a big one for Ben's cut. Maybe one for Mrs. D."

"Okay, let me help," Lerch said. He put some kind of stuff on the cut that made Ben twitch. Then he pushed a big bandage over the cut. "He's

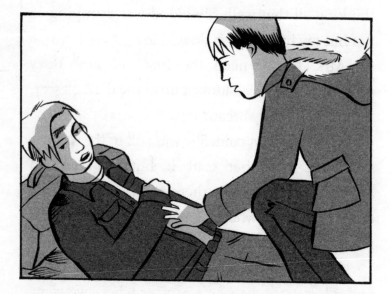

going to need stitches for something like that. And look at that bruise."

"What about Mrs. D?" I asked.

I think we were all afraid to lift her head. What if her face was smashed? What if she was dead?

It was Lerch who had the guts to check. He lifted her head from the steering wheel. We could see blood coming out of Mrs. D's nose. That was the bad news. And then we saw the good news — Mrs. D was breathing.

"Guys, we got a problem," Lerch whispered.

"Yeah, aren't you smart to figure that out," Rory snapped.

I had to force myself to think. It was all so bad, so awful, that my brain seemed frozen. But we had to make a plan. We had to do something. If Ben were okay, he would have told us what to do. He was our leader.

But Ben was out cold, so somebody had to take charge.

"Okay, listen up," I said. "Somebody is going to find us. Somebody is going to see where we went off the road. We just have to stay cool and wait for help."

"Yeah, that's good," Lerch said. "Except for two things — it's dark and there's a snowstorm. We could be stuck out here until morning."

"We'll freeze to death," Rory added.

"Besides, Ben and Mrs. D need help, like right away," Lerch added.

So much for my upbeat plan. The other guys were right — we had to do something right away.

And then we found a new problem. It was Rory who noticed it first.

"You guys smell something?" he asked.

I sniffed, and so did Lerch. Two sniffs and we got the bad news.

"It's gas," I said. "We've got to get out of here!"

"Move, move, move!" Lerch screamed.

CHAPTER 3

Up in Flames

The three of us could have gotten out pretty fast. The main door wouldn't open, but we could quickly make our way out the back. The back exit door would work for us.

But what about Ben and Mrs. D? We'd have to drag them over the seats. That might make their bleeding even worse.

"We better carry them," Lerch said. "This thing could blow up."

We didn't need him to remind us.

"Okay, let's get Ben out first," I told them. "I'll grab his arms and Lerch, you get his legs. Rory, you get that seat belt off Mrs. D — she's next. And find that fire thing."

"The fire extinguisher?"

"Yeah, find it — just in case."

I've never had to lift somebody who's out cold. I mean, I'm pretty strong for a 12-year-old. I can lift an 80-pound weight at school. But Ben must weigh 150 or so — and he wasn't helping.

I grabbed him under the arms and lifted. He came up from the stairwell, no problem. But then we had to get to the back of the bus. If the bus had been on its wheels, it would have been easy. But the bus was on its side. The only way to the back was by going along the windows.

"This guy is heavy," I said, grunting. "Give me some help."

It was awkward as anything. I pulled Ben while I slid backwards on the windows. I felt like a snail, crawling backwards — it was all so slow. Lerch got by Ben's feet and tried to push, but that didn't do

much good. He'd push, but Ben would just bend in the middle.

"Forget it," I told him. "I'll pull him by myself. Go help Rory with Mrs. D."

So I pulled — no, I dragged — Ben to the back of the bus. I could smell my own sweat and the gas from the bus. At one point, I bit my lip and I could taste blood. It was like metal, like iron, filling my mouth. But there was no time to stop and rest. I pulled and dragged, seat by seat.

There were 18 rows of seats. I got to count them, one by one. Each seat — each window — took me a little closer to the back. Then, finally, I was there.

"Hey, we made it," I told Ben. "We're gonna be okay."

Ben couldn't hear me — he was still out cold. So maybe I was trying to make myself feel better.

I pulled the red handle on the emergency door. The good news — it opened to the left. At least I wouldn't have to prop the door open with my back while I got Ben out. The bad news — there was a blizzard outside. The cold wind and snow blew into the bus as soon as I opened the door.

Lerch called from up front. "Hey, you trying to freeze us out?"

I didn't bother to answer. I pulled Ben up to the opening so I could grab his shoulders. Then I squeezed past him and jumped down into the snow. In two seconds, I pulled Ben through and dragged him away from the bus.

I was ready to go back in when I saw the other

guys. Lerch had dragged Mrs. D to the back, and she was at the emergency door. Behind them both was Rory.

"I'm over here!" I yelled to them.

Lerch jumped down, then pulled Mrs. D away from the bus. Rory came out last. He had the fire extinguisher and Mrs. D's coat.

"I've got to go back in," Rory said.

"You can leave your math book, you jerk."

"I need my coat," he said. "It's cold out here."

"Hey, it's not worth it . . . " I began, but Rory didn't listen. He jumped up on the door, then into the bus.

"Stupid . . . " I said, cursing.

I figure Rory was only in the bus for ten seconds when we saw the flames. They were up front, under the motor. At first, the flames were small. At first . . .

"Rory!" I yelled into the bus. "You've got to get out of there!"

Silence. I didn't know if Rory could hear me.

"I'll try to put out the fire!" Lerch yelled. He

was about to take off with the fire extinguisher when I grabbed him. It was a tackle, really. I learned how to tackle a guy when I played football. I grabbed his legs and Lerch fell face first on the ground.

"What the . . . " he snapped, but he didn't have time to finish.

With a soft *boom* the whole front end of the bus went up in flames. Then the fire began moving towards the back.

"Rory!" we screamed.

The seats burst into flame, row by row. We could see the fire moving towards us, fast.

"We've got to do something," Lerch cried.

But there was nothing to do — nothing we could do but watch.

Then we had a miracle. We saw Rory at the rear door.

"Jump, you idiot! Jump!"

We heard him coughing — and then he jumped. In a second, he was down on the snow.

We both ran to help him. Then the three of us

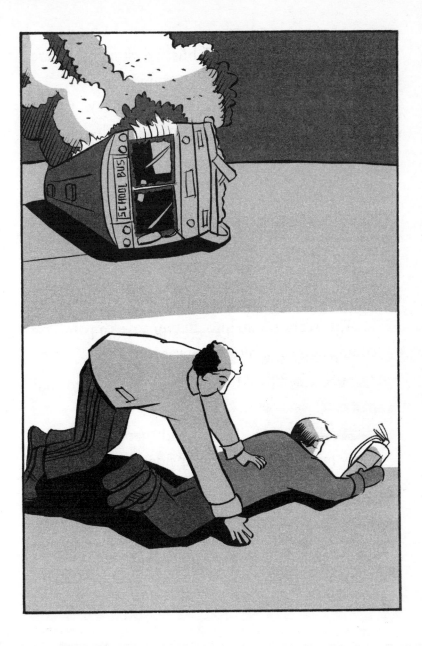

ran back away from the bus. We stopped where Ben and Mrs. D were on the ground.

"You could have got killed," I told Rory.

"Yeah, but at least I got my coat," he replied, smiling at me.

It was a strange moment. The school bus was going up in flames, but the heat and light from the fire made us feel better. Around us the snow was falling and the wind was howling. But in front of us was a fire, a little warmth. We were all alive and should have been grateful.

But Ben and Mrs. D were still in trouble.

"So what now, Craig?" Lerch asked me.

"We wait," I said. "Somebody is going to find us."

"Yeah, but Mrs. D is in bad shape," Rory said. "She might be bleeding inside. And Ben, he's bleeding outside again. I can't stop that with a bandage."

Lerch agreed. "It's getting cold, Craig. When the fire burns out, we're going to freeze."

I listened to them both and said nothing. They

were right. Things were bad. Things were going to get worse. But the first rule is always this — don't panic. Somehow we were going to get out of this. Somehow.

CHAPTER 4

What the . . . ?

We waited for ten minutes. The bus fire died out. In front of us was a burned hunk of school bus — yellow and black. Around us, the wind kept on blowing. Snow was falling in heavy flakes. The snow turned to steam when it fell on the bus. But the snow just made us cold.

"Craig, we can't just sit here," Lerch said.

"Somebody will find us," I told him.

"If somebody was going to find us, they would

have. They would have seen the fire and got here by now," Rory said.

I shook my head. "We've got to hang tough." It must have been a line I heard in some movie.

"Yeah, but I'm freezing," Rory said.

At least the four of us had winter coats. Mine was a thick parka that kept out the wind. Lerch had a hood on his coat that kept his head warm. Even Ben looked pretty warm in his parka. But Rory had a thin coat, a hand-me-down from his brother. And Mrs. D just had a bus driver jacket.

"Mrs. D is going to freeze," Lerch noted.

"None of us are going to freeze," I told them. "Somebody is going to see where the bus went off the road. Somebody had to see the flames from the bus. We just have to wait."

We sat there for another five minutes. I kept listening for a siren. I kept thinking that the cops would be looking for us. But there was nothing. We didn't even hear a car on the road above us.

"I'm going to climb up to the road," Lerch said suddenly.

"It's too steep," I told him.

"It beats sitting here."

In a flash, he was up on his feet and walking around the bus.

By now it was dark. If there was moonlight, we couldn't see it. There was nothing around us but blackness and snow. In a couple of seconds, we couldn't even see Lerch.

But in a minute, we could hear him.

"Sheeeesh!" A minute later, the same curse came our way, "Sheesh!"

Then Lerch was back beside us.

"Okay, the hill is too steep," he admitted. "I could do it in the summer, but there's ice under this snow."

Again we sat there. It's funny how cold gets into your bones. For the first little while, we were okay. The bus fire had kept us warm, and then our own bodies. But now the fire was gone and our bodies were getting colder. Rory's hands were freezing. My feet wouldn't get warm.

"This is crazy," Rory said at last. "We can't just sit here and wait to die! Ben is shivering. Mrs. D isn't going to last long. We've got to do something!"

"Just keep your cool," I shot back.

"I don't need cool — I'm cold already. I'm frozen!" he cried.

Just then, Ben twitched. He groaned, moved a little, and twitched again.

"Ben," I said, shaking him. "Ben?"

The twitching stopped and Ben just lay there

for a second. He coughed, blinked his eyes and then looked right at me.

"What the . . . ?" he said, his voice dry and groggy.

The three of us helped him sit up a little. He kept coughing, like the worst coughing fit you ever heard. I thought he might cough out his lungs.

"The bus . . . " he said. "I remember the bus . . . " Then he closed his eyes. Maybe he didn't want to remember what happened.

"We're in a little trouble, Ben," I told him. "The bus went off the road and down the hill. We thought that somebody would find us, but . . . well, I guess not."

"You think you can walk?" Lerch asked.

"Don't know," he groaned. "Help me up and we'll see."

In no time, the three of us got Ben up on his feet. He tried to take one step, but his leg was no good and he started to fall. We helped him up to try again, but the second try was no better.

"I think it's broken," he sighed. From the look

on his face, I could see how much it hurt him. "And I'm not breathing too good."

That might be the least of his problems. When Ben coughed, blood came up. When he lay on the snow, he shivered from cold. When he tried to move, pain shot through his body. He was hurt, like bad.

"Okay, I've got another idea," I said.

"I hope it's better than the last one," Rory snapped.

I ignored him. "I say we split up. A couple of us go for help. The other guy stays here with Ben and Mrs. D."

"Not bad," Rory replied. "Maybe your brain is working again, Craig. I saw a light over beyond the field. It's got to be a farmhouse or something."

Rory got up and looked into the distance, then I joined him. There was nothing out there.

"You sure you saw something?" I asked him.

"Yeah, pretty sure. The snow is really coming down now, but if we start walking that way, we'll find it."

"Okay," I said, my voice as firm as I could make it. "So who goes and who stays? Rock, paper, scissors — you ready?"

It was the old kids' game. Paper covers rock — scissors cut paper — rock breaks scissors. You play it with one hand, simple as that. I played against Lerch and won. My paper covered his rock. Then Lerch played against Rory. Rory's rock broke Lerch's scissors. The choice was made — Rory and I would go for help.

"It's the best way," I said, "since Lerch has the best parka and Rory knows where the light is. I'm giving Mrs. D my new scarf."

"She'll look just like a real fashion model," Rory laughed.

I ignored him. "Ben, you just take it easy and, like, stop bleeding." The bandage on his head was dark with blood.

"Yes, sir," he said, making fun of me.

"Rory, you ready?" I asked.

"Nothing like a nice walk in the snow," Rory replied.

CHAPTER 5

Into the Storm

The others huddled beside the burned-out bus. The warm metal broke the wind, so we put Mrs. D as close to the bus as we could. Then Ben and Lerch got in front of her.

"Got to share the warmth," Ben said.

"This is like a real close man-to-man defense," Lerch replied.

"Yeah, and you don't smell too good," Ben told him.

It was good to see the guys laugh. It was great to

see Ben joking, like he always did. Ben was still bleeding, but it seemed like the worst was over. We just had to find some help.

"How's Mrs. D?" I asked.

"Breathing," Lerch replied.

"Okay," I said, "you can see which way we're going. If somebody finds you first, tell them where to look for us."

Lerch looked off into the snow, then at us. "And if *you* find somebody, tell them we're tired of camping out by a burned-out bus."

I tried to smile. "Hang tight," I said. Then Rory and I turned from the group and headed off. By now there was a lot of snow on the ground. Rory walked in front because he'd seen the light. I walked behind him. We were going right into the wind.

In two seconds I knew we weren't dressed for this. We both had on winter coats, but neither of us had a hat or a hood. We didn't have gloves or even boots for our feet. We were dressed to ride a school bus, not to walk across a field.

My mom was always bugging me to wear a

hat. I never did. Even on a really cold day, I'd only put one in my pocket. But today I wished I had one. It was worth some major hat-head to keep warm.

After a minute, my running shoes were soggy and my head was freezing. I could see the wet snow building up on Rory's jacket. We both had our hands drawn up into our sleeves.

"Nice day," I shouted.

Rory said nothing. It was not day any more. I guessed that it was a little after six o'clock. Pretty soon, my mom would wonder where I was. My dinner would be getting cold on the table.

That reminded me — I was hungry and thirsty. We hadn't had a drink since the end of our game. When you start thinking about stuff like that, it bothers you. So I stopped. *Think about going forward*, I told myself. *Think about getting help.*

The snow was very heavy. The wind blew the snowflakes into our faces. It was hard to see, even hard to breathe. There was snot dripping from my nose.

"You see anything?" I yelled.

"Nothing," Rory yelled back.

Still we kept on walking. I think we went in a straight line. Rory said he had seen a light. We just had to get over the field and there'd be a house. Or a store. Or someplace warm.

After ten minutes, I was shivering. I tried to stop it. I pounded on my legs and on my arms, but I still shivered. The wind seemed to blow right through my track pants. Up ahead, there was a cap of snow on Rory's hair.

"Hey, Craig," Rory shouted back. "What's that thing you get in the cold? You know, when you're outside too long and get frozen."

"Hypo-something," I said.

"Yeah, well, I think I've got it."

"How come?"

"Because I'm shivering," Rory said.

"Shivering is good!"

"How's that?"

"It just means you're cold," I told him. "When you stop shivering, that's when you have to worry. Besides, we can't have that much farther to go."

Of course, I didn't know how much farther it was. At least the field was pretty even and flat. The wheat or peas, or whatever, had been cut close to the ground. The walking wasn't hard — except for the wind.

"Tell you what," I shouted, "I'll go in front. That will block the wind for you."

"Fair deal," Rory said.

Quickly he dropped behind me. Now it was my turn to break the trail. It was tough. The snow was deep and now it was slippery. I walked maybe twenty steps, then I slipped. I ended up flat on my back in the snow.

"Nice one," Rory said, helping me up.

Up front, the wind was worse. I could feel my cheeks, ears and nose starting to freeze. My nose and ears were the worst. They felt like they were burning. I tried to remember if this was good or bad, but my brain was blank.

After five minutes, I put my sleeves up to cover

my ears. But then my balance was off. I felt myself getting dizzy and I knew that wasn't good.

Then Rory fell down. I heard him shout "Hey!" as he slipped, so I turned to help him.

But Rory just lay there in the snow. He was shivering and breathing funny.

"Come on," I said, "I'll help you up."

"I don't want to get up," he told me. The words came out all slurred. *I don wanna geddup.*

"We've got to keep going," I told him.

"I wanna sleep."

"You can't sleep," I shouted. "We've got to find that house. We've got to get help."

But Rory just lay in the snow. This was bad. When you get really frozen, you start to give up like that. You shiver and get dizzy and give up. And then you freeze to death.

So I bent over him and grabbed his sleeves. "Get up, you jerk," I shouted at him. "I can see the house!" That was a lie, but I had to do something.

"You can?" Rory asked.

"Yeah, just come with me," I told him.

So I got Rory moving again — with a lie. There was no light up ahead, nothing. But I knew we had to keep moving. If we just lay down, we'd be dead.

"We're almost there," I said, lying some more.

Rory didn't say a thing. We just kept moving forward — towards nothing. The snow swirled in the wind. The dark night made the world all black with white flecks. There was nothing — nothing at all.

Until I saw a dark shape.

CHAPTER 6

Fire in the Darkness

In front of us was a house, an old farmhouse. The place looked like no one had lived in it for years. The paint was long gone. The windows were busted. Maybe it was a good house, like forty years ago. Now it was just a big, junky shack.

But even a shack was better than nothing.

"It's a house," I shouted to Rory.

"But there's nobody there," he said.

"Who cares? It'll get us out of this wind," I told him.

We climbed up on the old porch and I pushed at the door. It was locked. I looked over at the windows. Going in over broken glass would be dumb.

So I kicked at the door. One, two, three kicks. At last the latch broke. The door popped open and we went inside.

Rory was still shivering, and he was still very weak. But he would be better out of the wind. The only problem we had now was darkness.

The old farmhouse was really dark. It was blacker than night. I had to go in slowly, like a blind man. I felt my way into the first room. Maybe it was the living room. Rory came right after me.

"Now can I sleep?" Rory asked. His words were still slurred.

"No, we've got to make a fire."

"Yeah, sure," he said. Then he plopped down on the floor. I could hear his body sink down. "You make the fire. I'm gonna sleep."

I could have turned and forced him up. I could have slapped him in the face. But I let him sit down on the floor. Maybe it was the best thing.

I felt my way to the back of the house. I figured the kitchen would be at the back, and I was right. The trouble was — it *used* to be a kitchen. Now it was a bunch of broken cupboards and a busted table.

I needed some matches. If I was lucky, maybe there'd be some matches on a shelf.

I felt all over the shelves. I went into each cupboard. There was dirt and mouse turds and crud, but no matches.

Think, I told myself. *You've got to think.*

The trouble was — it was hard to think. When you're freezing, it's hard to keep your head straight.

No matches, I said to myself. *Not in the kitchen.* But maybe someplace else. I bet teenagers come in here to party. They come to smoke and drink. Maybe, someplace . . .

So I felt my way back to the first room. I felt along two walls, then came to a fireplace. *The teenagers would party around here*, I said to myself. So I felt around the fireplace, then along the floor.

I knocked a book off a shelf. Then I felt some old newspapers on the floor. I kept feeling around. I could hear mice running across the floor. The last thing I wanted to do was touch a mouse.

Then I felt something round and plastic. A lighter! Someone had left a cheap lighter.

I said a little prayer. I don't do that much, but it seemed the right time for one. *Please, God, let this thing work.* I put an *Amen* at the end and gave the lighter a flick.

A spark. That was a start. I shook the lighter a little, then flicked it again. A spark and a little flame . . . and then it was out.

Thank you, God, I said to myself.

But I couldn't waste the flame. Next time, I had to be ready. I found the book on the floor and ripped out some pages. Then I pulled a shelf off the wall for some wood. The shelf was old and broke in half when I smashed it over my knee.

I hit the pieces against the stone floor. The wood broke again, and a sliver stuck in my finger.

I piled up the pages in the fireplace, then put

some slivers on top. I got the bigger wood ready.

By then, my hands were shaking from the cold. *Okay, do it,* I told myself. I flicked the lighter but didn't get a spark. I had to flick it faster. I blew on my fingers to try to warm them up. I shook the lighter and my hands to get them ready.

This time I got a spark, then a little flame. My hands were shaking as I moved the lighter over towards the paper . . . but the flame went out. *Got to keep the little tab pressed down.* Rory was freezing to death. I couldn't mess up again.

Flick, flick, hold the flame. Slowly I moved the lighter and got one piece of paper to catch on fire. Then I pushed another piece to touch that flame. And then another.

Okay, I've got a paper fire, I told myself. A paper fire is good for maybe a minute. Now I had to get the wood going.

I fed the slivers into the burning paper. One would light, then die out. I pushed in another, then a bigger one. Slowly my fire grew. At last I put in the shelf pieces and they caught hold. Now I had ten minutes worth of fire.

I also had light. I looked around the room for something else I could burn. There were more newspapers in one corner. There was even an old wooden chair!

In a second, I had smashed the chair into pieces. I fed the pieces into the fire. Slowly I got a nice blaze going. I warmed my hands. For a second, I felt good.

"Hey, Rory," I called out. "We're going to make it. We've got a fire. We're going to be okay."

I heard nothing.

"Rory, I said we'll be okay. Rory!"

I looked back into the room, but Rory wasn't there.

CHAPTER 7

Now What?

So *now what?* I asked myself.

Rory might have gone off someplace in the house. Maybe he'd fallen asleep in one of the other rooms. Maybe he'd gone outside.

I had to have some light. I rolled up some newspapers, then touched them to the flames in the fireplace. It made a torch, kind of. But my torch wouldn't last long.

I went back to the kitchen . . . nothing.

"Rory! Rory, you jerk! We've got a fire!" I screamed.

I looked into the room at the right of the stairs . . . nothing. Could Rory have gone upstairs? Nah, I would have heard him.

But now my newspaper torch had burned out.

I went back to the outside door. In no time, I pushed it open and yelled.

"Rory! Are you out there?"

The only sound that came back was the wind. The cold cut through me, just as it had before. I closed the door and got back to the fire.

Now you've really got to think, I told myself. Rory was gone. My friends Ben and Lerch were out in the storm, waiting. They needed help, and fast.

But I was okay. The fire was starting to warm me up. I had enough wood to keep it going all night. In the morning, the storm would be over. In the morning, I could go out and find help.

But in the morning, the others would be dead.

So I really had no choice. I had to keep going. I had to find the light that Rory had seen. I had to

find a real house, with somebody who could help my friends. But this time I'd be smarter.

I took off my parka, and then my sweatshirt. Boy, then I was cold! I took a piece of broken glass and cut one arm from my sweatshirt. Then I put the sweatshirt and parka back on.

I warmed my hands in front of the fire. Then I warmed up the arm of my sweatshirt and tied it around my head. I took a few pages of the old newspapers and stuck them under my coat and down my track pants for extra padding.

Not bad, I said to myself. I should have thought of this before. If only my running shoes weren't so wet, I'd almost be warm.

Before I left, I figured I should do one more check for Rory. I went around the whole first floor calling his name.

"Rory! Rory, where are you?"

There was one last place to check — upstairs. This made me really nervous. The whole house was blowing in the wind. The stairs weren't in very good shape. I might get upstairs and just fall through the floor.

So I went up real slow, one step at a time.

"Rory, are you up there?"

I had just reached the top of the stairs when I heard a strange sound. It seemed to come from outside. It was a roar, like the wind, but deeper.

And it was getting louder.

Now I was really scared. I was alone in this old house. Something strange was going on outside — or maybe inside the house.

I don't believe in ghosts. I don't believe in any

of that stuff. But the sound was very strange, and then there were a few footsteps. I swear, I heard footsteps.

"Rory?" I asked, my voice all high and scared.

I was shaking at the top of the stairs. Something was coming. Something was pounding at the door.

Then the door flew open. A dark shape came in, covered with snow. It looked like a monster, or something like that. The monster stopped, looked at the fire, then looked up at me.

At last the monster spoke. "You trying to burn my house down?"

CHAPTER 8

Who's the Hero?

Rory had gone off to save my life.

While I was trying to set a fire, Rory had looked out the window. He'd seen the real farmhouse. He'd gone off to that farmhouse, despite the storm. That's how we got saved.

When the farmer came to find me, Rory was already in a warm bed. The police were coming to help the others.

In no time, I was back at the farmer's new

house, drinking some soup. My feet were getting warm by the fire.

Rory came down the stairs from a bedroom. He saw me at the fire and sat down, a blanket wrapped around him.

"It's hypothermia," he said.

"What?"

"The word we couldn't think of back in the field. It's hypothermia. It makes you shiver and then your brain doesn't work so well."

"So what's the treatment?" I asked.

"Get wrapped up, get warm, drink soup. Just like we're doing." Then he sat down beside me at the fire.

Of course, we all had to be checked out. I was fine and Rory was pretty good. The doctors were worried about him, but he came up okay.

Lerch came out perfect. The moral of the story — wear a parka with a hood. At least when your bus crashes. Or else listen to your mom and wear a hat.

Ben needed stitches to his head. He also had a broken leg and broken ribs. So much for the rest of his basketball season.

Mrs. D had lost some blood, but she wasn't too bad. A few days in the hospital and she came out just fine. She writes letters to the paper now. She thinks all school buses should have ABS brakes. I think she's right.

Rory and I are having a debate. He says that I'm the hero. It's because I stopped him from getting killed in the burning school bus. I say that he's the hero because he found the farmhouse. At school, all the kids think we're both heroes.

As for the team, we had a really bad season. Without Ben, we just couldn't score. And maybe we were a little scared when we had "away" games. You never know where a school bus might end up in a snowstorm.

Bats Past Midnight
by SHARON JENNINGS

Sam and Simon wonder about a fancy car that hangs around their school late at night. When they try to find out more, they end up in trouble at school, at home and with the police.

Three Feet Under

by PAUL KROPP

Scott and Rico find a map to long-lost treasure. There's $250,000 buried in Bolton's mine. But when the school bully steals their map and heads for the old mine, the race is on.

Choose Your Bully

by LORI JAMISON

Sam and Richard have a great idea to deal with their school bully — hire a bodyguard. But when their bodyguard starts to bully them, they have to get smarter.

Paul Kropp is the author of more than fifty novels for young people. His work includes nine award-winning young adult novels, many high-interest novels, as well as books and stories for both adults and early readers.

Paul Kropp's best-known novels for young adults, *Moonkid and Liberty* and *Moonkid and Prometheus*, have been translated into many languages and have won awards around the world. His illustrated books for younger readers include *What a Story!* and four books based on Mr. Dressup characters. His high-interest novels have sold nearly a million copies in Canada and the United States. For more information on Paul, visit his website at www.paulkropp.com.